Margaret Wise Brown's

GOOD

BOOK

Addison-Wesley Publishing Company, Inc.
Reading, Massachusetts 01867
L.C. No. 43–15137
ISBN: 0-201-09155-0
Printed in U.S.A.

JK-WZ-798

A CHILD'S
NIGHT

Illustrated by Jean Charlot
Young Scott Books

Night is coming.
Everything
is going to sleep.
The sun goes over
to the other side
of the world.

Lights turn on
in all the houses.

It is dark.

All the little birds
stop singing
and flying
and eating.
And they tuck
their heads
under their wings
and go to sleep.

Sleepy birds.

The little fish
in the darkened sea
sleep with their eyes
wide open.

Sleepy fish.

The sheep in the fields
huddle together
in a great warm blanket
of wool.
The lambs stop leaping,
the rams stop ramming,
the sheep stop *baaa-ing,*
and they all go to sleep.

Sleepy sheep.

The wild monkeys
and the wild lions
and the wild mice
all close their eyes
in the forest.

Sleepy wild things.

The little sailboats
furl their sails
and are tied up
at their docks
for the night.

Quiet sailboats.

And the cars and trucks
and airplanes are all
put in their houses—
in dark garages
and hangars.
Their engines stop.

Quiet engines.

The little kangaroos
jump in their mothers'
warm pouches
and close their eyes.

Sleepy kangaroos.

The purring pussy cats
blink their eyes.
Then their eyes close,
and they stop purring.

Sleepy pussy cats.

The bunnies close
their bright
red eyes.

Sleepy bunnies.

The clovers are cold
in the fields.
The bees stop
their buzzing
and fly into
their hives.

Sleepy bees.

The squirrels
are hidden
in the trees.

Sleepy squirrels.

The children
stop thinking
and whistling
and talking.
They say their prayers,
get under their covers,
and go to sleep.

Sleepy children.

Dear Father,
hear and bless
Thy beasts and
singing birds,
And guard with
tenderness
Small things
that have
no words.